BOOKS BY LAURA (L.A.)MARIANI

Untamed Hearts

The BAD Boy

The BAD Girl

Holiday Romance

14 Days to Love Series: Short Sweet Steamy

Parisian Serendipity

Venetian Whispers

Mumbay Surprise

Romeo in Rome

New York Melody

Artic Embrace

Santorini Sunsets

Havana Heat

Barcelona Dreams

Marrakesh Magic

Vienna Waltz

Sydney Sparks

Amsterdam Affair

Cape Town Safari

Box Set

14 Days to Love: Short Sweet Steamy

Twelve Days of Christmas Series

A Partridge in a Pear Tree: Hot Spicy Christmas Novella

Two Turtle Doves: Hot Spicy Christmas Novella

Three French Hens: Hot Spicy Christmas Novella

Four Calling Birds: Hot Spicy Christmas Novella

Five Golden Rings: Hot Spicy Christmas Novella

Six Geese a-Laying: Hot Spicy Christmas Novella

Seven Swans a-Swimming: Hot Spicy Christmas Novella

Eight Maids a-Milking: Hot Spicy Christmas Novella

Nine Ladies Dancing: Hot Spicy Christmas Novella

Ten Lords a-Leaping: Hot Spicy Christmas Novella

Eleven Pipers Piping: Hot Spicy Christmas Novella

Twelve Drummers Drumming: Hot Spicy Christmas Novella

Box Set

Twelve Days of Christmas

Shadowbrook Paranormal Series

A Halloween Romance: Enchanted in Shadowbrook

The Midnight Hour:A Halloween Shadowbrook Romance

Navy Seals Hunks Series

SEALed Hearts

SEALed with a Kiss

SEALed Undercover

SEALed Pursuit

SEALed Love Code

SEALed beyond Duty

Box Set

Navy SEAL Hunks

A Royal Romance Trilogy

A Coronation Weekend Romance

The Wicked Princess

The Lost Kingdom

Box Set

A Royal Romance Trilogy

The Nine Lives of Gabrielle Series

Gabrielle (prequel/first in series)

For Three She Plays

A New York Adventure

Searching for Goren

Tasting Freedom

For Three She Strays

Paris Toujours Paris

Me Myself and Us

Freedom Over Me

For Three She Stays

London Calling

Back in Your Arms

The Greatest Love

Box Sets

For Three She Plays - Book 1-3

For Three She Strays - Book 4-6

For Three She Stays - Book 7-9

The Nine Lives of Gabrielle Book 1-9 + 3 Bonus stories

Box Set - Italian Edition

Le Nove Vite di Gabrielle: Libri 1-9 + 3 Bonus

THE BAD BOY

UNTAMED HEARTS
BOOK 1

LAURA (L.A.) MARIANI

PEOPLE
ALCHEMIST

ISBN: 978-1-917104-16-6

FOREWORD

The Bad Boy is a OTT insta-love steamy romance novella that is intended for a mature audience. If you crave a fast-paced, passionate read, jump right in!

Next in the series - **The Bad Girl.**

PROLOGUE

The razor glides across my jaw, a sharp contrast to the rough stubble that's been my companion for the last few weeks. I stare into the mirror, watching the tattoos that ink my skin stretch and shift with every movement. They're more than just art; they're a map of my life.

The buzz of anticipation outside my trailer is like a pulse, the Heartland Speedway coming alive in the dusk. I can almost taste the raw energy of the crowd, hungry for the roar of engines and the thrill of speed. But for me, these pre-race events are nothing but a necessary evil—a dance I'd rather not indulge in.

Every cheer from the stands, every flash of a camera—it's all part of the game, and I play it because I have to, not because I want to.

· · ·

"Keep it short," I mumble, the words bouncing off the metal walls. Get in, show face, get out. No lingering, no unnecessary risks. The echo of betrayal still rings too loud in my ears, the memories, the accident. The ghost that refuses to be outrun.

I splash water on my face, the cold a stark reminder that I'm here, present, and as much as I hate it, bound to this circuit of spectacle and scrutiny. Tonight, I'll be the king they all expect—the alpha atop his throne of horsepower and heartbeats. And when it's done, I'll vanish back into the night.

"Nothing's gonna go wrong," I say.

With a final glance at the tattoos marking my journey, I turn away from the mirror. Time to face the floodlights and the frenzy. Time to be what they all came to see.

1

OH LORD

I fidget nervously with my clipboard as I survey the crowded event space, my chest tight with anxiety. This is my first big event planning gig, all on my own. I am all gussied up for the occasion with my little Sunday best dress. I've checked and double-checked every detail, but I can't shake the feeling that something might go wrong.

Especially with him here. Ryan Blake.

Even just thinking his name sends a shiver down my spine. I've heard the rumors about his awful reputation - his arrogance, his drinking, using and abusing women, and spitting them out like used handkerchiefs. Yet, they go back for more.

And then the accident ... Yes, THE accident.

. . .

Part of me dreads having to deal with him. And part of me ... I shake my head, trying to clear away those inappropriate thoughts.

"Focus", Sophie. You have a job to do. I glance at my watch - he should be here any minute now.

My eyes scan the entrance, my heart pounding faster with each passing second. Where is he? I hope he'll show up on time for once. This event has to go off without a hitch if I want to prove myself and secure this promotion.

Suddenly, the chatter hushes as if all the oxygen has been sucked out of the room. I follow everyone's stares to the door and-

Oh, my goodness. There he is.

Ryan Blake strides in like he owns the place, all dark charisma and raw masculinity. His very presence is electric, charging the air. I forget how to breathe.

Our eyes lock across the room, and I freeze, transfixed.

I can feel his eyes on me. The heat of his gaze is like a physical touch, intense and unrelenting. He smirks, holding my gaze a beat too long. Boldly undressing me with his eyes, a wolf stalking his prey.

. . .

His presence fills the space, dominating it like he owns every inch. Up close, he's even more devastatingly handsome than described. Tall, tattoed, chiseled features, hypnotic eyes, an aura of untamed power—I feel it deep in my core.

I flush all over, knees weak. The rest of the room fades away until it's just us, the pull between us magnetic and undeniable.

I swallow hard. Oh Lord, please help me, I'm in trouble...

Focusing on my breath, I straighten my spine and walk towards him, chin held high. I won't let him intimidate me.

"Mr. Blake, I'm Sophie Mitchell. Welcome ..." I extend my hand, wishing I could hide my trembling fingers. He doesn't take it right away, just stares down at me, eyes simmering.

"Sophie," he drawls in that sinfully deep voice. The way he draws out my name sends shivers down my spine, and I almost melt into a puddle on the spot.

"Shall we?" I say, more to myself than him, gesturing towards the ... ahem ... the ... damn. He steps so close I can smell his scent, a heady mix of leather and woodsmoke.

.   .   .

"Mr. Blake," ahem ... ahem, "we do have a schedule to keep." I try to sound assertive, but my voice betrays my nerves.

His smirk widens. "Ryan," he corrects.

The evening unfolds in a blur of handshakes and small talk, but my thoughts drift back to Ryan's heated gaze. I should be repulsed by everything he is. Instead, my panties are soaked, my nipples hardening against the fabric of my modest dress. What is happening to me? This is sinful ... he is certainly not 'The One' I have been waiting and saving myself for. His words echo in my mind, unleashing a desire I never knew existed.

"Sophie," I hear . "How about a dance?" It is Blake whispering in my ear and holding my elbow, pulling me to face him. "I promise I won't bite... until you beg me to."

"I don't dance with the likes of you," I hiss, trying to tug my arm free. I need to escape before it is too late. But he only tightens his grip, seemingly enjoying the way my pulse jumps beneath his fingers.

"You can't fight this, sweetheart," he smirks, undeterred, "I can see how much you want me."

.   .   .

What an insufferable so-and-so.

"You're delusional," I snap, annoyed. But my body betrays me, swaying closer, my breathing shallow. "I'm not one of your race track groupies."

"No, you are not," he leans in some more. "But deep down, you're aching to surrender completely. Live a little, sweetheart."

I pull back, shaking my head. "I can't do this. I won't." My voice quivers. "Now, if you'll excuse me, I have work to do."

2

LOVING AN ANGEL INSTEAD

The evening is even more tedious than usual, and everyone wants a piece of me. Amidst a sea of debauchery, she is a vision of purity. The way she moves and smiles politely at the sponsors is captivating.

An angel.

Weaving through the crowd, I make my way over, my eyes never leaving her delicate face. She senses my approach and turns, her sky-blue eyes widening slightly as they meet mine.

My gaze caresses her form and travels slowly down her conservative floral dress, barely concealing a pair of large gorgeous puppies, the tiniest waist, and the most gorgeous ass I have ever seen before returning to her flushed cheeks. My heart is pounding in my chest.

. . .

Sophie, her name is Sophie.

I reach out and grab her elbow, my fingers curling around it possessively. She jumps at the sudden contact, her pink lips parting in surprise. I want to devour that pretty mouth. I can see the fear in her eyes and a hint of excitement. I lean in closer, my lips brushing against her ear as I speak.

"Come dance with me, Sophie. Just one dance." She hesitates, her eyes widening before she composes herself. Her voice is like a gentle breeze, but there's a steeliness to it that catches my attention. My hand slides down to the small of her back, pulling her closer to me until our bodies are pressed together. She softens against me for a moment, her resistance crumbling under my touch. But then she pushes away, placing a firm hand on my chest. Her eyes turn to molten embers as anger builds up within her, a tight clench of her jaw and a fiery glint in her gaze.

"No," she says firmly. "I won't be another name on your list of conquests, Ryan Blake." She trembles under my touch, torn between desire and self-control, I can sense the pull towards me, the yearning in her body. She wants to give in, let go of all inhibitions, and lose herself in the moment with me.

I feel the heat radiating off her as she stands before me, and I want nothing more than to be consumed by it. But then she pulls away, her voice wavering but resolute. "I can't do this. Not now, not ever." There's a fierce determination in her stance as she turns to leave, hips swaying with an irresistible rhythm.

I watch her go, and my blood is running hot. This isn't over. Not by a long shot.

Frustration gnaws at my insides as I march back to my trailer, a busty blonde clinging onto my arm.

"Baby, I want you so much," she whispers, her hand caressing my biceps. But as soon as we enter the dimly lit space, I push her away and pace around the room, my mind consumed with thoughts of Sophie.

And now, here she is, standing naked in front of me, but all I can think about is Sophie's soft curves and delicate features. What is happening to me?

"Get out of here," I say.

"Baby," she says, fiddling with the zip of my trousers.

"Get the fuck out of here before I throw you out," I shout picking up her clothes from the floor and tossing them in the street.

"Bastard," she yells, "you fucking bastard."

. . .

I collapse onto my bed, gripping my throbbing cock in my hand as I lose myself in fantasies of Sophie. For the first time in years, it was someone else's image that fuels my desire - a woman I had just met.

Sleep finally overtakes me, but it brings no rest. Instead, I'm plunged into the nightmare that haunts my every sleeping hour.

There she is, Monica's alluring curves and dark hair spilled over Derek's body as they writhe in a passionate embrace. My heart pounding with jealousy as the green-eyed monster consumes me. Suddenly, I'm behind the wheel of my car, the rage fueling my actions as I press down on the gas pedal. The sound of screeching tires fills the air, followed by screams and a sickening crunch as Derek's body is crushed under the weight of my vehicle.

I jolt awake, my body drenched in sweat, but the memory of that fateful day just as vivid.

Sophie is my angel and my salvation; I know it. Now, I just need to make sure she's mine.

3

I WANT YOU. I WANT YOU NOT

"Sophie?" His voice cuts through the soft hum of mingled conversations, sending shivers down my spine. It is the first time we meet again.

"Mr Blake," I reply, trying to keep my tone level and professional. "I didn't know you were interested in PR events."

A smirk plays on his lips. "I'm interested in anything that involves you." His words are laced with an edge, making my heart race.

I swallow hard, feeling trapped under the weight of his stare. I've been trying to avoid him, but fate has other plans.

"Is that so?" I manage to say, feigning disinterest, but my body betrays me. I'm drawn to him, to the danger that lingers in his piercing eyes, to the strength evident in his tattooed arms.

"Abso-fucking-lutely," he says, closing the distance between us in a few confident strides.

I back up a step, bumping into the edge of a table. Ryan's too close, his scent—leather and adrenaline—wrapping around me, intoxicating and overwhelming.

"Mr Blake, I..." My protest dies on my lips as he leans in, his breath warm against my ear.

I should push him away and tell him I'm not the kind of woman who gets involved with men like him. But my resolve crumbles as he places his hand on the small of my back, possessive and sure.
    "Ryan… angel."

"Ryan, we can't—" I begin, but he silences me with a finger to my lips.

"Can't or won't?" he challenges, his eyes locked onto mine.

The question hangs heavy in the air. Can't because it's against everything I stand for, I'm waiting for marriage. Won't because deep down, I'm terrified of the power he holds over me, of the way my body yearns for his touch.

. . .

"Both," I whisper, hoping to sound more convincing than I feel.

He smiles, a predatory flash of teeth. I'm playing with fire, and I know it. But as Ryan walks away, leaving me flustered and wanting, I realize the battle is far from over, and I'm unsure how much longer I can resist.

The next day, I'm standing by the track, the roar of engines vibrating through my bones. I grip the rail in front of me, the metal cool and firm beneath my fingers—a stark contrast to the heat building inside me as I watch Ryan's car glide over the asphalt like a sleek predator.

The moment Ryan appears, stepping out of his car, helmet under his arm, his gaze finds mine instantly. It's magnetic, that pull, and I can't look away. His strides are confident, each step a silent claim, as if he owns the ground he walks on—and, God help me, every inch of space in my head.

"Enjoying the view?" he asks, his voice low and certain, a siren's call that resonates with something wild within me.

"Trying to understand the fascination," I manage to quip, feigning indifference. But my voice betrays me, a fluttering timbre that speaks of attraction rather than curiosity.

. . .

He chuckles, and the sound is dark chocolate—smooth, rich, impossible to resist. "It's all about control, Sophie. Power." His eyes lock onto mine. "Dominance."

A shiver cascades down my spine, an involuntary response to words that should send me running. He's danger incarnate, a man whose mere presence demands submission.

"Sounds... overwhelming," I whisper, my pulse racing, my inner voice screaming that this isn't me, that I'm not one for reckless abandon or for men who speak in terms of ownership.

"Only if you're afraid of letting go." His smirk tells me he knows exactly what effect he has on me.

But I am afraid. I am so scared of the raw intensity in his eyes, the unspoken promise that he could unravel me with a touch, stripping me of the composure I cling to so desperately.

"Maybe I am," I admit, my confession a whisper lost in the din of the Heartland Speedway.

He steps closer, invading my space, making my breath hitch. "It means you have something worth losing yourself in."

· · ·

My cheeks flush with heat, my body betraying my mind's stern warnings. He's too much. Too close, too intense, too everything.

"Ryan," I breathe out, a plea for reason I know won't come.

"Say my name again," he commands, touching my arm lightly.

"Ryan," I repeat, softer this time, my defences crumbling like the walls of a sandcastle at high tide.

"Good girl," he murmurs, approval lacing his tone, and I hate how much I crave his praise. "There's power in surrender, Sophie. Let me show you."

God help me, I want him to.

With a deep breath, I tear my eyes away from his and start to walk away. My legs tremble with anticipation and excitement, but I know that I can't cave in this easily. I have my principles to uphold, after all.But as I feel his strong hand grabbing my wrist, I know I am lost.

He spins me around, and his eyes are on fire. "Do you really think you can just walk away from me, Sophie?" he growls, his voice low, dangerous, and oh-so-irresistible.

·   ·   ·

"You can't just-" I protest, but my words are cut off as his lips crash onto mine, stealing my breath. His hands are everywhere, molding me to his hard, muscular body, and I can't help but melt into him.

With a growl of desire, he hoists me up, and my legs automatically wrap around his waist, my arms around his neck. He walk us towards a nearby private tent, our mouths still fused together in a heated kiss.

Breaking away for a moment, he growls, "I've been dreaming about this since I laid eyes on you."

Before I can even respond, his lips are back on mine, and his hands are roaming my body, cupping my breasts, squeezing and kneading them through my dress. I arch into his touch, moaning into his mouth, unable to control the intense desire coursing through my veins.

"I want you, all of you," his voice thick with need.

Oh Lord, what am I doing? This is wrong, so wrong ...

"No, stop ..." I plead, on the verge of tears, "Please, Ryan, stop." Ashamed, I run away.

4

NO MORE DANCING

The roar of my own heart drowns out the revving engines as I watch her, my entire world narrowing down to her shaking form. But fuck me, I need her. I can't stop thinking about her. The prudish act, the way she blushes so easily drives me wild. I know I'm not good for her; I've got more demons than she can handle, but I can't stay away.

"Sophie," I growl, my voice low and dangerous as I stalk towards her, pushing other people out of my way like they're nothing more than inconvenient obstacles. "We need to talk."

She spins around, those big doe eyes brimming with unshed tears, for me or for herself, I don't care. I've had enough of this dance we've been doing. "Ryan, please-"

• • •

"No!" I cut her off, grabbing her wrist in a vice-like grip. "You're coming with me, and you'll listen."

She tries to wriggle out of my grasp, but I'm having none of it. I'm done with her prudish bullshit, her holier-than-thou routine.

I bundle her into my car, slamming the door shut with a satisfying thud. The engine roars to life, the vibrations resonating through my very core. I floor it, my anger fuelling every movement.

We pull up at her apartment, a nondescript little box in a sea of sameness. I follow her inside, slamming the door with enough force to rattle the cheap IKEA frames on the wall.

"Ryan, what the hell do you think you're doing?" she hisses, her chest heaving with fury and fear.

"This," I growl, and before she can blink, I've backed her up against the wall, pinning her with my body. "This is what I think I'm doing."

Her breath catches in her throat, and I can smell her arousal over the faint scent of vanilla wafting from her hair. Her nipples harden against her blouse, betraying her true desires.

. . .

"Ryan, please," she whimpers, arching her hips against me.

"No more 'please,'" I rasp in her ear, tracing my tongue along her delicate earlobe. "Tonight and every night after, you're mine, Sophie. And I'm going to show you exactly what that means."

With that, I crush my lips to hers, kissing her with a fervor that leaves no doubt about my intentions. Her resistance crumbles like the cheap drywall around us, and she melts into my arms, a moan escaping her pink lips.

I tear away her clothes, revealing her luscious curves hidden beneath the conservative facade. Her pink cotton panties are soaked, and I growl my approval, ripping them off before sliding my fingers into her wet heat.

"Oh, Ryan," she moans, her back arching like a cat in heat.

As I wrap my arms around her, her sweet scent overwhelms me and sends a jolt of electricity through my body. Now is the time. Her skin is soft against my hands as I run them down her curves, feeling the goosebumps rise at my touch. My fingers trace along the edge of her pink lace bra, teasingly outlining the perfect shape of her breasts.

"I've been yours since we first met." Lowering my lips to hers, I claim them in a passionate kiss before trailing down her throat and murmuring into her ear, "And now I'm going to claim your body as mine."

I fumble with the clasp of her bra, finally ripping it apart. Her breasts spill out into my hands, soft and supple. I drop to my knees in front of her, taking her left nipple into my mouth and swirling my tongue around it until it hardens against me. She tastes like warm honey, and my mouth waters for more.

Her fingers tangle in my hair as I suck on her nipples, my own desire growing with each moan she lets out. My hand travels up her thighs, feeling the wetness between them and pulling another whimper from her lips. The smell of her arousal fills my senses, and I know I need to taste her.

With a swift movement, I lift her up and carry her over to the table, determined to make her mine.

"Sit," I command and spread her legs wide. I press a finger into her slick entrance, causing her to gasp and arch her back. But one finger isn't enough. I add another, struggling to fit them both inside her tight, wet hole.

My thumb rubs circles over her swollen clit, making her whimper and writhe under my touch. Her hands grip the edges of the table as she leans back, offering herself entirely to me. It's an intoxicating sight. I push a third finger inside of her, pumping them in and out while massaging her clit with my thumb. She's so close, but so am I.

. . .

"You're so beautiful," I breathe as I run my calloused fingers over her exposed skin.

""Ry- an, I … I've never - " she starts to say, "I'm a virgin." As soon as the words left her lips, I could feel my own arousal building even more.

"I know, but tonight, that changes," I growl. "Tonight, you're mine."

My angel. My virgin angel.

I need to be inside of her, to make her mine in every way possible. I drop to my knees and dive between her spread legs. My tongue eagerly laps at her juices, savoring her taste as my fingers plunge into her tightness. With each flick of my tongue and pump of my fingers, I give myself a firm stroke, feeling my own desire grow with hers. And then she cries out, her body convulsing as she reaches the peak of pleasure. Her sweet release floods into my mouth, mixing with my own primal need for her.

The scent of her arousal fills the air: I flip her over onto her hands and knees on the table. Her tight pink asshole puckered as I run my cock teasingly over it, eliciting moans and shivers from her body. With one hand reaching around to find her slippery folds, I use my tip to slide over her entrance. The heat and tightness is like a fire inside my cock; I need to be inside her now.

"Hold onto the table, angel," I command, again positioning myself at her entrance. She gasps as I push into her, struggling to accommodate my size. "You're too big," she whimpers, "it hurts" but I know she would get used to it. I lean down and brush her hair off her back tenderly before sliding myself in deeper.

"Relax, and let me take care of you," I reassure her as she limps against the table. "Ryan," she whines, overwhelmed by the sensation. "I …I can't … take you."

"Hush, sweetheart," I soothe, pushing myself in.

With each thrust, her body tenses, and her moans grow louder as I struggle to control my own urges.

"Ryan," she begs, the intensity in her voice pushing me closer to the edge. But I can't give in just yet. I need to take her slow despite the overwhelming desire to pound into her with all my might.

"Relax for me," I whisper. And then I feel it - the release of her tight grip on me, telling me she wants this just as much as I do. "Let me in, let me fuck your tight pussy," I murmur, teasing her with my words and relishing how her body responds.

. . .

As she struggles to catch her breath, I can feel her hips pressing against mine, urging me deeper into her. Each time she gasps out my name, the heat intensifies. My fingers grip her hips tightly as I thrust harder and faster, making her moan and writhe beneath me.

"Does it feel good, Sophie?" I growl in her ear as I press my mouth to her neck, leaving marks of possession on her skin. "Do you like being claimed by me?" Her response is a loud cry, and I know she does.

With every stroke, I leave no doubt that she belongs to me and no one else. The sound of our bodies colliding echoes in the room. And when my hand grazes over her puckered asshole, she cries out even louder.

"Say my name, Sophie," I demand as I thrust deep into her once again. "Louder. Every time I fuck you." She screams my name as our rhythm becomes more frantic and primal.

"That's it, angel," I pant as I continue to claim her with each thrust. "Whose pussy is this? Who owns you?"

"Yours," she cries out in response as pleasure courses through us both. And in that moment, nothing else matters.

. . .

My thumb works its way into the folds of her pink hole, teasing her sensitive flesh as my dick thrusts in and out of her slick pussy. My hands roam down her body, cupping and squeezing her breasts as her breaths grow shallow and ragged. I can feel myself nearing the edge.

"Come for me, baby. Let me hear my name on your lips when you come." She screams my name over and over as I continue to thrust into her tightness, feeling it pulsing and tightening around me. Finally, she falls over the edge, and I let myself go too. A wave of pleasure crashes over me as I release inside of her, marking her with my seed and claiming her as mine. She utters my name one last time before collapsing onto the table in exhaustion. I gently pull out of her warm embrace and carry her to the bedroom, laying her down on the bed and tucking her tired body between the sheets.

As I wrap my arms around her, I whisper, "You're mine now, Sophie. No matter what happens, you'll always be mine." And as we drift off into sleep together, I know she is my angel.

"I need you, Sophie. Run away with me."

EPILOGUE

I press my foot harder on the accelerator, guiding the sleek sports car through the barren wasteland of the Nevada desert. Like my life, this drive is about speed, adrenaline, and control. But today, it isn't just the engine purring that has my heart racing. No, it is my baby in the passenger seat.

I knew she was mine from the moment our eyes met a few days ago. She is an angel in a den of sin, and today, she is mine in every sense of the word, and the knowledge sends a possessive thrill through my veins.

One hand steady at the wheel, I command, "Open your legs," and she obeys without hesitation. I glide my other hand between the crease of her thighs, finding her already soaking wet for me. She gasps, her head thrown back in ecstasy as I tease her swollen clit with nimble fingers. Her sweet scent fills the car, an intoxicating mix of desire and innocence.

. . .

"You're mine now, Mrs Blake," I growl, my voice a guttural rasp. "Mine to touch, mine to taste, mine to possess."

I can't believe she said yes.

She trembles beneath my touch, her hips grinding in time with my movement. "Yes," she moans, her voice hoarse with need, surrendering completely to me. "Yours... yours alone."

With two fingers, I penetrate her tight heat, relishing in the way she clenches around me like a vise. She was untouched until last night, and the thought alone drives me wild. I want to consume every inch of her, mark her as mine forever. Her first, her last.

"Ryan," she cries out, her body arching towards me. "I-I ... I'm going to... oh, God!"

With a final, hard thrust of my fingers, I send her over the edge, her body shuddering under my touch. Her climax is like a symphony, her cries of ecstasy blending with the roar of the engine.

As her tremors subside, I pull the car to the side of the road and then lean over, capturing her swollen lips with mine, my tongue pillaging her mouth as ruthlessly as my fingers had just pillaged her core. Sophie belongs to me and only me.

She has awakened something in me I never knew existed, a hunger so fierce it consumes me. Today, we've claimed each other in the neon-lit chapel in Vegas, but tomorrow, I can chase down the one thing that has eluded me for so long with my angel by my side: redemption.

GET YOUR FREE EBOOK

Sign up the Laura (L.A.) Mariani mailing list for a FREE steamy romance.

You'll be the first to hear about new releases, exclusive offers, bonus content and all Laura's news. You can even email her back. She loves chatting with her readers!

To claim your free ebook visit:
https://laura-mariani-author.ck.page/freeshortstory

AUTHOR'S NOTE

Thank you so much for reading **The Bad Boy**.

I hope you enjoyed the story. A review would be much appreciated as it helps other readers discover the story. Or a few stars perhaps - the more the better ;-) !

Thanks.

Laura xx

ABOUT THE AUTHOR

Laura Alexandra (L.A.) Mariani is a best selling author of Short & Steamy Romance |Where Alpha Males Meet Fierce Heroines for Sweet Endings, your go-to author for captivating romance tales that will sweep you off your feet and keep you on the edge of your seat!

When Laura is not weaving stories of love, desire and suspense, you'll find her exploring the vibrant streets of London, drawing inspiration from its hidden corners and bustling markets, or strolling through the charming streets of Paris, savoring street food in Rome, or relaxing on a sun-kissed beach in Bali, her journeys fuelling her creativity and infuse her stories with wanderlust.

You can also follow her on

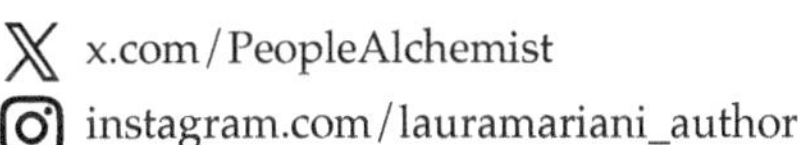

X x.com/PeopleAlchemist
instagram.com/lauramariani_author

www.ingramcontent.com/pod-product-compliance
Lightning Source LLC
Chambersburg PA
CBHW070454170726
48291CB00005B/1756